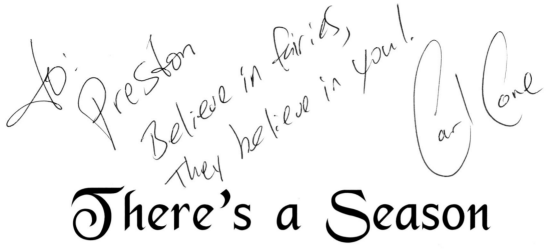

To: Preston
Believe in fairies,
They believe in you!.
Carl Cone

# There's a Season
# For All

Written By:

## Sammy Shu

Illustrated By:

## Carl Cone

Text copyright © 2005 by Sydney S. Cone
Illustrations copyright © 2005 by Carl Cone
Published by Raynestorm Books, an imprint of Silver Rose Publishing Inc.

Library of Congress Control Number: 2006921735

ISBN 0-9778211-0-2

Manufactured under the direction of **Double Eagle Industries.**
For manufacturing details, call **888-824-4344**, or email to
**info@publishingquest.com**

Printed in China

There are a group of people I'd like to dedicate this book to,
without whom it never would have been written.

Jill & Scott:
Thank you for giving me a year at home with my babies.
It was then that I wrote this beautiful story.

Rayne, Stormy & Bella:
My babies. You are my inspiration.

Joey:
I've never written anything without bouncing the idea
off of you first. Thank you just doesn't seem to cover it.

To the love of my life:
Never quit creating. You're better than you think you are.

A long time ago, before people lived in houses, there was a very special place called "Tween Land".

The name meant a place between the real and the imaginary. It was a wonderful place to be and that is why a lot of fairies lived there.

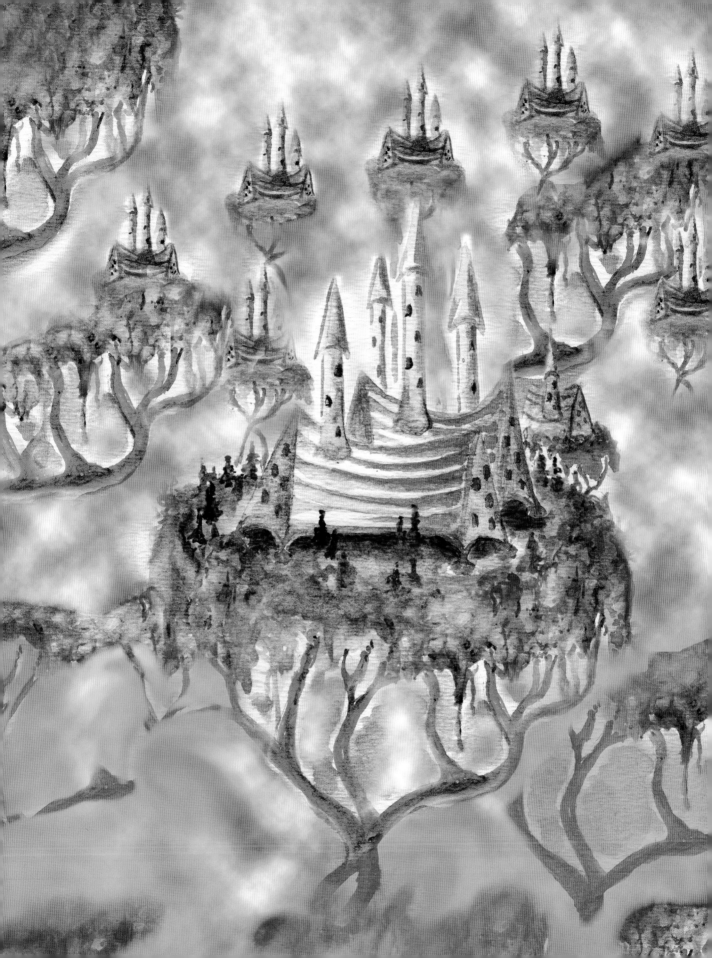

The queen of the fairies was a beautiful and wise fairy who loved all of her followers very much. Everyone loved the queen and they loved her four beautiful and sweet daughters even more. The four princesses had been born just hours apart but they were all very different. They had been lovingly guided by a strong mother and had learned all there was to know about ruling the kingdom of Tween Land.

Winter was the oldest of the four and the leader in most situations. She had hair the color of fresh unblemished snow and eyes that put the clear blue sky to shame. Her skin was kissed with just a touch of rose as though the wind had brushed her once too often.

Spring was in love with life.
She enjoyed every aspect of living.
Her older sister Winter thought that Spring
was sometimes frivolous but Spring didn't
care. She was happiest chasing bees and
smelling the flowers.
Pink was the word that best described her.
Wonderful shades of pink from the tips of her
toes to the top of her head, broken up only by
the violet of her expressive eyes.

Summer was the most outgoing of the four. She always had something fun planned and was great at talking others into joining. She had hair as yellow as the blossom of a sunflower and eyes the color of green healthy grass. Her skin was darker than her sisters', accenting her striking hair and eyes. Everyone who saw her, forever remembered the combination.

Fall was the youngest of the four sisters'. She was also the brightest of them. Sometimes Fall would plan huge festivities for the children in the kingdom. These were always the best and most well-planned parties and festivals. Everyone knew which sister was the smartest. Fall's beautiful long hair was the color of the ripest of oranges and she had huge milk chocolate colored eyes.

Those eyes always looked as if they knew something that no one else did.

The princesses were the most beautiful
fairies in the land and all of the people
knew them well.
The kingdom was thriving and all was
as it should be.

The sisters' grew older and in their eighteenth year the queen was ready to pass the running of the kingdom over to her children. She had become too old to handle everything.

Like most rulers at the end of their reign, she went to rest in the Land of Imagination.

In the beginning, all went well and combining their strengths worked.

Winter was very strong physically and emotionally. Fall was the organizer. Summer could always find the silver lining around any cloud, while Spring kept love and laughter in all their lives.

This combination worked... for a while.

Then a problem arose. You see, one of the most important of the sisters' jobs was to control the environment. They got to decide if it would be cold or hot, whether it would rain or snow, what plants would grow and for how long they would live.

With all of the sisters' controlling these things together, their kingdom became chaotic.

Winter liked it best when there was snow on the ground, icicles hanging from bare trees, frost in the air and lakes so cold that they had become solid.

Spring liked it best when it rained; feeding the plants and making them grow. She loved to let the warm water wash over her while imagining that she was a pink tulip waiting to be born.

Summer liked it best when it was hot, when the sun would beat down and warm your skin. She liked it when the water was warm enough to swim in and her wings would glisten with moisture and sunbeams.

Fall liked it best when the trees were changing, preparing for the cold. She thought this was a beautiful transformation, when all the leaves would turn to shades of yellows and oranges.

Because of their inability to work together,
all of their favorite things were happening
at one time.
This created a huge problem.
Just as a flower would bloom, a frost would
come and kill it.
A glorious snowflake would form and the rays
of the sun would melt it before it came to rest
on the ground.
Just as the leaves of a tree would grow in all
of their green glory, they would begin to change
to a more earthy color.

All of this chaos distressed the entire kingdom. There was never enough time to enjoy anything before it changed into something else. The princesses began to argue over who had the best ideas and for the first time ever there was strife in Tween Land.

Winter decided that this couldn't go on. She called her sisters together and asked them to try and come up with a way to solve the problem. At first this seemed like a bad idea. They all felt very strongly that each of their ideas were the best. This caused many hours of arguing until Fall came up with a great idea.

Her plan was to break up the year into four equal parts and they would take turns making everything just the way they liked it. The other sisters' would help during each turn to make all go smoothly.

This was such a wonderful idea that they all agreed immediately. The only question was, who would go first and how would they explain their decision to the people?

After much discussion, they decided that they would call these separations during the year "seasons". They would be named after the sister that was in charge and the order would be decided by age.

d Fall.

Winter went first because
she was the oldest;

Spring was next,

Then Summer...                           and Fall.

Soon the kingdom was once again without strife. The princesses had learned how valuable each of them was in their own way. The kingdom of Tween Land lived in all of its seasonal glory... happily ever after.

# ABOUT THE AUTHOR

Sammy Shu lives and works in Denver Colorado. She and her family spend many an hour enjoying the beautiful countryside. Her appreciation for the fantastic is evident within her stories. They are beautifully woven with realistic situations while remaining true to her childlike imagination.